The Brave Tin Soldier

and other stories

Miles
KeLLY

First published in 2011 by Miles Kelly Publishing Ltd
Harding's Barn, Bardfield End Green, Thaxted, Essex, CM6 3PX, UK

2 4 6 8 10 9 7 5 3 1

Publishing Director Belinda Gallagher

Creative Director Jo Cowan

Editor Amanda Askew

Senior Designer Joe Jones

Production Manager Elizabeth Collins

Reprographics Anthony Cambray, Stephan Davis, Lorraine King, Jennifer Hunt

ISBN 978-1-84810-497-6

Printed in China

British Library Cataloguing-in-Publication Data
A catalogue record for this book is available from the British Library

ACKNOWLEDGEMENTS
Artworks are from the Miles Kelly Artwork Bank

Cover artwork by Rupert van Wyck (Beehive Illustration)

Every effort has been made to acknowledge the source and copyright holder of each picture.
Miles Kelly Publishing apologises for any unintentional errors or omissions.

Made with paper from a sustainable forest
www.mileskelly.net
info@mileskelly.net
www.factsforprojects.com

Contents

The Rebellious Titans and Gods 4

The Treasure Stone of the Fairies . . 12

Bucephalus 20

Gilgamesh and Humbaba 27

The Brave Tin Soldier 34

The Rebellious Titans and Gods

An ancient Greek myth

BEFORE THE BEGINNING of time, there was nothing but an emptiness called Chaos. Out of the darkness emerged three beings who became known as Gaea, Tartarus and Eros.

Gaea, the earth goddess wished for some company, so she gave birth to Uranus, the god of the sky, and he surrounded her on all sides. Next, the mountains and the sea sprang from Gaea, shaping the landscape of the world.

Soon, Gaea and Uranus created three children together – giants, each with fifty heads and one hundred arms! Shortly after, three more children were born to them – again giants. But this time, they each had just one eye in the middle of their forehead. They came to be known as the Cyclopes.

With such immense strength and power, Uranus became fearful that the children would eventually try to overthrow him and take control of the universe themselves. So one by one, Uranus seized them, throwing them down into the depths of Tartarus, the underworld, from where they could not possibly threaten him.

Furious and devastated, Gaea began to hate Uranus for his cold-hearted, ruthless actions. With time, she gave birth to thirteen more children – the immortal Titans. Among them were the god of the sun Helios, the goddess of the moon Selene, the god of the waters Oceanus, the goddess of prophecy Themis, the strongest Titan Atlas, and finally Prometheus – the most intelligent Titan, who created the human race out of soft clay.

Yet Gaea's bitterness towards Uranus only increased with time. The day came when she put a mighty, curved sickle into the hands of her youngest Titan son,

Cronus. "I want to punish your cruel father and free your brothers and sisters from their underground banishment," she explained. "If you kill your father, you can rule in his place."

His eyes gleaming greedily, Cronus did what he was told. Across the universe echoed his father's cries of agony. Rivers of blood flowed from his wounds, and from this stream of wickedness sprang forth three evil creatures, the Furies, and a race of terrifying warrior giants.

Being immortal, Uranus couldn't die, so Cronus threw his father's body into the ocean. "Now I reign over all things!" Cronus roared.

To Gaea's despair, Cronus proved to be just as much of a tyrant as her husband. Relishing his control over the universe, he refused to free the hundred-handed giants and the Cyclopes from Tartarus.

Outraged, Gaea warned, "Your cruelty will come full circle! The day will come when your children will destroy you, just as you have destroyed your own father."

Cronus simply sneered. In his arrogance, he thought that he could cheat the prophecy. He would make sure that he had no children. If he had none, then how could they vanquish him?

Cronus was married to his sister, Rhea. In due course, a baby daughter Hestia was born. Cronus didn't hesitate in swallowing her whole. To Rhea's horror and misery, Cronus did exactly the same with their next four babies – Demeter, Hera, Hades and Poseidon. By the time Rhea was due to give birth to their fifth child, her heart was breaking with grief. She went to Gaea and begged for help. "Mother," she sobbed, "how can I fool Cronus, so I can keep my baby? I can't stand to lose another!"

Gaea eagerly came up with a plan. She hid Rhea away in a mountainside cave on the island of Crete. There, unseen, Rhea gave birth to a baby boy called Zeus. Rhea left Zeus in Gaea's care, and hurried home. Then she wrapped a rock in a blue blanket and presented it to Cronus. "Here is your newborn son!" she proclaimed. Cronus didn't spare a second to look at the infant. He simply opened his jaws and gulped

the bundle down. Smirking with satisfaction, he thought of how he had defeated his destiny once again...

And so, unknown to his father, Zeus grew up safely into a strong, courageous god. When he came of age, he disguised himself as one of Cronus' servants and waited. Then, when one day Cronus called for a drink to be brought to him, the disguised Zeus carefully took him a chalice of sweet-tasting poison instead.

In one gulp, Cronus drained the drink – and immediately realized that something was wrong. Clutching and clawing at his stomach, cramps and spasms stabbed inside him. Suddenly, up came the rock he had swallowed, followed by Poseidon, Hades, Hera, Demeter and Hestia – who were all fully grown ... and furious!

"Behold your son, Zeus, and all your other children!" Rhea said proudly. "They are ready to rule in your place, with justice and wisdom, instead of cruelty and tyranny. Your fate has come!"

"You will regret this because this means war!" bellowed Cronus, striding away to prepare for battle.

While Cronus was rousing all the other Titans to fight at his side, Zeus sped down to Tartarus with his brothers and sisters to release the hundred-handed

giants and the Cyclopes. Of course, the monsters were so grateful that they pledged their allegiance to the gods and goddesses and vowed to fight with them. Then the Cyclopes presented Zeus and his brothers with special gifts to help them in their mighty task. To Zeus, they gave the weapons of thunder and lightning. To Poseidon, they gave a magic trident for stirring up sea-storms and creating earthquakes. To Hades, they gave a helmet of invisibility.

It was now time for the gods and goddesses to return to the upper world and begin the battle.

Enraged, the Titans were ready and waiting, forming a formidable flank behind Cronus. With blood-curdling war cries, they flung themselves forwards across the heavens into the attack.

As the Titans advanced, the hundred-handed giants tore great chunks of rock off the mountains and hurled them at the enemy. The two sides clashed together, in an embroiled mass of arrows, spears and swords. The blows of the mighty warriors made the earth tremble and shake until the awful rumblings were heard down in the depths of Tartarus itself. The cries and groans of the injured echoed around the mountains and across the heavens. And still the Titans and the gods fought, inflicting terrible wounds on each other. As immortals, none of them could die.

When Zeus unleashed his ear-splitting thunderclaps and blinding lightning bolts, the stench of smouldering flesh filled the air as the Titans were set alight. While the Titans threw themselves into the sea, trying to quench the burning flames, the hundred-handed giants saw their chance. Seizing the howling Titans one by one, the giants dragged them below the earth down to the underworld. There, they bound them in the strongest of chains and left them for all eternity.

How the victorious gods and goddesses rejoiced! At last, tyranny had been overthrown and they would rule together, spreading fairness and heroism throughout the universe. The gods decided upon their kingdoms – Hades won the underworld and became the king of the dead. Poseidon won the sea and became lord of the oceans. And Zeus won the sky, and became ruler of the world. All three leaders determined not only to keep peace and harmony among immortal beings, but also to teach humans how to live prosperous lives – to respect their fellow people, all other living creatures, and above all, the gods themselves.

Contented, the gods and goddesses made their own home on Mount Olympus. And there they have ruled ever since.

The Treasure Stone of the Fairies

By William Elliot Griffis

LONG AGO, when London was a village and Cardiff only a hamlet, there was a boy who tended sheep on the hillsides. His father was a hardworking farmer, who every year tried to grow out of the stony ground some oats, barley, leeks and cabbage. In summer, he worked hard, from the first croak of the raven to the last hoot of the owl, to provide food for his wife and baby daughter. When his boy was born, he took him to the church to be christened Gruffyd, but everybody called him 'Gruff'.

In time, several little sisters came to keep the boy company. His mother always kept her cottage, which was painted pink, very neat and pretty, with vines

12

covering the outside, while flowers bloomed indoors. These were set in pots and on shelves near the latticed windows. They seemed to grow finely, because so good a woman loved them. The copper doorframe was kept bright, and the broad borders on the clay floor, along the walls, were always fresh with whitewash. The pewter dishes on the sideboard shone as if they were moons, and the china cats on the mantelpiece, in silvery lustre, reflected both sun and candle light. Daddy often declared he could use these polished metal plates for a mirror when he shaved his face. Puss, the cat, was always happy purring away on the hearth, as the kettle boiled to make the sour oat jelly, which daddy loved so well.

Mother Gruffyd was always neat, with her striped apron, her high peaked hat, with its scalloped lace and quilled fastening around her chin, her little short shawl, with its pointed, long tips, tied in a bow, and her bright red petticoat folded back from her frock. Her white collar and neck cloth knotted at the top, and fringed at the ends, added fine touches to her picturesque costume.

In fact, young Gruffyd was proud of his mother and he loved her dearly. He thought no woman could be quite as sweet as she was.

Once, at the end of the day, on coming back home, from the hills, the boy met some lovely children. They were dressed in very fine clothes, and had elegant manners. They came up, smiled, and invited him to play with them. He joined in their sports, and was too much interested to take note of time. He kept on playing with them until it was pitch dark.

Among other games, which he enjoyed, had been that of 'The king in his counting house, counting out his money,' and 'The queen in her kitchen, eating bread and honey,' and 'The girl hanging out the clothes,' and 'The saucy blackbird that snipped off her nose.' In playing these, the children had aprons full of what seemed to be real coins, the size of crowns, or five-shilling pieces, each worth a dollar. These had 'head and tail,' beside letters on them and the boy supposed they were real.

But when he showed these to his mother, she saw at once from their lightness, and because they were so easily bent, that they were only paper, and not silver.

She asked her boy where he had got them. He told her what a nice time he had enjoyed. Then she knew that these, his playmates, were fairy children. Fearing that some evil might come of this, she charged him, her only son, never to go out again alone, on the mountain. She mistrusted that no good would come of making such strange children his companions.

But the lad was so fond of play, that one day, tired of seeing nothing but byre and garden, while his sisters liked to play girls' games more than those which boys cared most for, and the hills seeming to beckon him to come to them, he disobeyed, and slipped out and off to the mountains. He was soon missed and a search was made for him.

Yet nobody had seen or heard of him. Though inquiries were made on every road, in every village, and at all the fairs and markets in the neighbourhood, two whole years passed by, without a trace of the boy.

But early one morning of the twenty-fifth month, before breakfast, his mother, on opening the door, found him sitting on the steps, with a bundle under his

arm, but dressed in the same clothes, and not looking a day older or in any way different, from the very hour he disappeared.

"Why my dear boy, where have you been, all these months, which have now run into the third year?"

"Why, mother dear, how strange you talk. I left here yesterday, to go out and to play with the children, on the hills, and we have had a lovely time. See what pretty clothes they have given me for a present."

When she tore open the package, the mother was all the more sure that she was right, and that her fears had been justified. In it she found only a dress of white paper. Examining it carefully, she could see neither seam nor stitches. She threw it in the fire, and again warned her son against fairy children.

But soon, after a great calamity, both father and mother changed their minds about fairies.

They had put all their savings into the venture of a ship, which had for a long time made trading voyages from Cardiff. Every year, it came back bringing great profit to the owners and shareholders. In this way, his father was able to eke out his income, and keep his family comfortably clothed, while all the time the table was well supplied with good food. Nor did they ever turn from their door anyone who asked for food.

But in the same month of the boy's return, bad news came that the good ship had gone down in a storm. All on board had perished, and the cargo was totally lost in the deep sea, far from land. In fact, no word except that of dire disaster had come to hand.

Now it was a tradition, as old as the days of King Arthur, that on a certain hill a great boulder could be seen, which was quite different from any other kind of rock to be found within miles. It was partly imbedded in the earth, and beneath it, lay a great, yes, an untold treasure. The grass grew luxuriantly around this stone, and the sheep loved to rest at noon in its shadow. Many men had tried to lift, or pry it up, but in vain. The tradition, unaltered and unbroken for centuries, was to the effect, that none but a good man could ever budge this stone. Any and all unworthy men might dig, or pull, or pry, until doomsday, but in vain. Till the right one came, the treasure was as safe as if in heaven.

But the boy's father and mother were now very poor and his sisters now grown up wanted pretty clothes so badly, that the lad hoped that he or his father might be the deserving one. He would help him to win the treasure for he felt sure that his parent would share his gains with all his friends.

Though his neighbours were not told of the

generous intentions credited to the boy's father, by his loving son, they all came with horses, ropes, crowbars, and tackle, to help. Yet after many a long days' toil, between the sun's rising and setting, their end was failure. Everyday, when darkness came on, the stone lay there, as hard and fast as ever. So they gave up.

On the final night, the lad saw that his father and mother were holding hands, while their tears flowed together, and they were praying for patience.

Seeing this, before he fell asleep, the boy resolved that on the morrow, he would go up to the mountains, and talk to his fairy friends about the matter.

So early in the morning, he hurried to the hill tops, and going into one of the caves, met the fairies and told them his troubles. Then he asked them to give him again some of their money.

"Not this time, but something better. Under the great rock there are treasures waiting for you."

"Oh, don't send me there! For all the men and horses of our parish have been unable to budge the stone."

"We know that," answered the principal fairy, "but you should try to move it. Then you will see what is certain to happen."

Going home, to tell what he had heard, his parents had a hearty laugh at the idea of a boy succeeding where men, with the united strength of many horses and oxen, had failed.

Yet, after brooding for a while, they were so dejected, that anything seemed reasonable. So they said, "Go ahead and try it."

Returning to the mountain, the fairies, in a band, went with him to the great rock.

One touch of his hand, and the mighty boulder trembled, like an aspen leaf in the breeze. A shove, and the rock rolled down from the hill and crashed in the valley below.

There, underneath, were little heaps of gold and silver, which the boy carried home to his parents, who became the richest people in the country round about.

Bucephalus

By James Baldwin

OLD PHILONICUS of Thessaly was the most famous horse-raiser of his time. His stables were talked about from the Adriatic Sea to the Persian Gulf, and many of the best war steeds in Greece and Asia Minor had been bred and partially trained by him. He prided himself particularly on his 'ox-headed' horses – broad-browed fellows, with large polls and small, sharp ears, set far apart. Proud creatures these were, and strong, and knowing, and high-spirited – just the kind for war steeds; and that was about all that horses were valued for in those days.

Among these 'ox-heads' there was one which excelled all others in courage, beauty, and size, but which, nevertheless, was a source of great concern to his master. He seemed to be altogether untamable, and, although he was now fourteen years old, there was not a horseman in Greece who had ever been able to mount him. He was a handsome creature – coal-black, with a white star in his forehead. One eye was grey and the other brown. Everybody admired him, and people came great distances to see him. Had Philonicus been less shrewd, he would have sold him for half the price of a common steed, and been glad that he was rid of him. But, like most men who spend their lives among horses, he knew a thing or two. He kept the horse's untamableness a secret, and was careful that only his good points should be exhibited. Everybody who had any use for such an animal wanted to buy him.

"What is the price?"

"Thirteen thousand dollars."

That answer usually put an end to the talk. For, as an ordinary horse might be bought at that time for about seventy dollars, and a thoroughbred war steed for two hundred, who was going to pay such a fabulous price? Half a dozen fine houses could be built for that money. There were rich men who made Philonicus some very handsome offers – a thousand dollars, five thousand, eight thousand – but he held steadily to his first price,

and the longer he held to it the more anxious everybody became to buy.

At last, however, after the horse had reached middle age, shrewd Philonicus got his price. King Philip of Macedon, who was ambitious to become the first man of Greece, was the purchaser; and Philonicus, after hearing the gold pieces jingle in his strong-box, led the great Bucephalus up to the Macedonian capital and left him safely housed in the king's stalls. He was careful, no doubt, to get back into his own country before Philip had had time to give the steed any kind of examination.

You may imagine what followed. When the horse was brought out upon the parade ground for trial the skilfullest riders in Macedon could not mount him. He reared and plunged, and beat madly around with his sharp hoofs, until everybody was glad to get safely out of his reach. The greatest horse-tamers of the country were called, but they could do nothing.

"Take him away!" cried the king, at last, in great rage. "That man Philonicus has sold me an utterly wild and unbroken beast, under pretense of his being the finest horse in the world; but he shall rue it."

But now Bucephalus would not be led away. The horse-tamers tried to throw ropes over his feet; they beat him with long poles; they pelted him with stones.

"What a shame to spoil so fine a horse! The awkward cowards know nothing about handling him!" cried the king's son, Alexander, who was standing by.

"Are you finding fault with men who are wiser than yourself?" asked the king, growing still more angry. "Do you, a boy twelve years old, pretend to know more about handling horses than these men, whose business it is?"

"I can certainly handle this horse better," said the prince.

"Suppose you try it!"

"I wish that I might."

"How much will you forfeit if you try, and fail?"

"I will forfeit the price which you paid for the horse," answered Alexander.

Everybody laughed, but the king said, "Stand away, and let the lad try his skill."

Alexander ran quickly to the horse and turned his head toward the sun, for he had noticed that the animal was afraid of his own shadow. Then he spoke softly and gently to him, and kindly stroked his neck. The horse seemed to know that he had found a friend, and little by little his uneasiness left him. Soon with a light spring the lad leaped nimbly upon his back, and

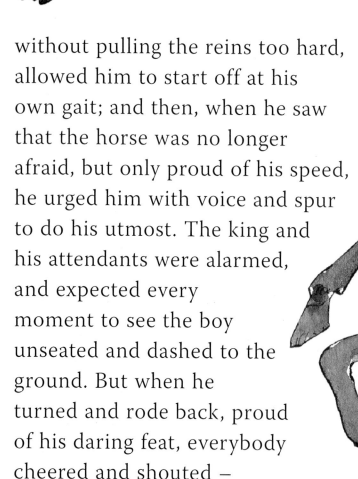

without pulling the reins too hard, allowed him to start off at his own gait; and then, when he saw that the horse was no longer afraid, but only proud of his speed, he urged him with voice and spur to do his utmost. The king and his attendants were alarmed, and expected every moment to see the boy unseated and dashed to the ground. But when he turned and rode back, proud of his daring feat, everybody cheered and shouted – everybody but his father, who wept for joy and, kissing him, said: "You must look for a kingdom which is worthy of you, my son, for Macedonia is too small for you."

After that, Bucephalus would allow his groom to mount him barebacked; but when he was saddled nobody but Alexander dared touch him. He would even kneel to his young master, in order that he might mount more easily; and for sixteen years thereafter he served him as faithfully as horse ever served man. Of course, he was with Alexander when he conquered Persia, and he carried him into more than one hard-fought battle. At one time (I think it was in Hyrcania) he was stolen; but his master made proclamation that unless he were forthcoming within a certain time, every man, woman and child in the province should be put to death, and it was not long before he was brought back.

In the great battle that was fought with King Porus, of India, Alexander recklessly rode too far into the enemy's ranks. The horse and his rider became the target for every spear, and for a time it seemed as if neither could escape. But the gallant Bucephalus, pierced by many weapons, and with streams of blood flowing from his neck and sides, turned about and, overriding the foes which beset them, rushed back to a place of safety. When he saw that his master was out of danger and among friends, the horse sank down upon the grass and died.

Historians say that this happened in the

year 327 BC, and that Bucephalus had reached the good old age – for a horse – of thirty years. Alexander mourned for him as for his dearest friend, and the next city which he founded he named Bucephalia, in honor of the steed that had served him so well.

Gilgamesh and Humbaba

From the epic poem *Gilgamesh*

GILGAMESH WAS A MIGHTY king, ruler of the great city of Uruk. His father, Lugalbanda, had been a noble king before him and his mother was the wise goddess Ninsun. Gilgamesh was especially favoured by the gods. The great mother goddess Nintu had helped to create him. The sun god Shamash had bestowed beauty upon him. The storm god Adad had filled him with courage. The god of learning and intelligence Ea had given him wisdom. Indeed, Gilgamesh had been granted many divine gifts, but he had not been given the gift he prized most of all – immortality. Gilgamesh was human, and like all humans, he would eventually die.

One day, Gilgamesh was sitting with his dearest friend, the warrior Enkidu, when he declared, "Before I die, I want to win a place among the greatest heroes who have ever lived. Then, people will tell tales of my glorious deeds for thousands of years to come, and my name shall live on through the ages."

"O great Gilgamesh," Enkidu replied, "you are already a renowned ruler of a powerful people and a magnificent city, admired throughout the land. How do you intend to achieve even greater fame? Surely you are as famous as you can be!"

Gilgamesh paused. There was an excited gleam in his eyes. He announced, "I am going to slay the giant, Humbaba!"

Enkidu gasped. "Tell me you are not serious! Everyone who has heard of Humbaba quakes in fear at his name! Humbaba has a ferocious face like a great dragon, a terrifying roar like a rampaging river, gnashing teeth like a bloodthirsty lion, and fiery breath that scorches everything in his path. The divine ruler

Enlil appointed Humbaba to scare travellers away from the mountain home of the gods, which lies in the deep, dark Cedar Forest of Lebanon – so wild and treacherous that you can enter it and never find your way out again."

"All that is true," smiled Gilgamesh. "Nevertheless, I am determined to track this monster down and slay him! The whole world will talk of my adventure. Say you will come with me, Enkidu."

Enkidu shook his head. "My lord, I am not yet ready to die," he exclaimed.

"Come, Enkidu," coaxed Gilgamesh, "would you rather wait for death to find you, or go out and greet it face to face. I am going to slay Humbaba. Poets will sing forever more of Gilgamesh, King of Uruk!"

Enkidu sighed. "My king, if your mind is made up, then I shall remain at your side until the very end."

Gilgamesh hurried off to prepare. First, he made a sacrifice at the temple of Shamash. "O radiant one," he begged, "take pity on my mortality. Help me to conquer Humbaba and win everlasting fame."

Then Gilgamesh called the elders of Uruk to a meeting and informed them of his plan. They were horrified and protested angrily, but Gilgamesh was defiant and could not be persuaded otherwise.

Finally, he told his mother of his plans. She wept and wailed, and prayed to the gods to change his mind. But finally, she kissed Gilgamesh and Enkidu goodbye. "Go forth with my blessing, but return safely home to me."

Gilgamesh took the bravest warriors of Uruk, along with supplies and weapons, including a mighty axe especially forged by his smiths for felling Humbaba. Then Enkidu led the way out of the high gates of Uruk and down the road that led towards Humbaba's lair.

To reach the gateway to the Cedar Forest of Lebanon, it should have taken six weeks of marching night and day. However, with motivated hearts, Gilgamesh, Enkidu and the warriors covered the distance in only three days. Before they entered the eerie gloom of the woods, Gilgamesh gave a stirring speech. "No one who follows me should be afraid. If we die, we die making lasting names for ourselves. We will not disappear into the well of time and be forgotten, like cowards. So be of good courage and let us go forward together!"

"Gilgamesh's dreams prophesy victory!" announced Enkidu. "Our mighty god Shamash will help us, and we will triumph over the greatest of giants, Humbaba!"

Then Gilgamesh, Enkidu and their brave army plunged determinedly into the forest, their hearts pounding. They marched all day into its depths, before Gilgamesh gave the order to stop. He took out his axe and began cutting down one of the massive cedars – a bold ploy to attract Humbaba's attention.

In the silence of the forest, the thudding chops resounded like the beat of a battle drum. As the tree finally toppled and fell, the warriors saw bursts of flame in the distance and heard huge footsteps striding towards them. Humbaba's thunderous voice struck terror into their hearts. "Who dares enter my forest and cut down the trees of the heavenly mountain of the gods? Answer me and prepare to die!"

"I, Gilgamesh, King of Uruk, have felled your tree," Gilgamesh bellowed back, "and now I will fell you with my mighty axe!"

Gilgamesh brandished his axe overhead and charged forwards to meet the oncoming monster. Enkidu roared a mighty battle cry, and he and the warriors

followed suit. As they did so, Shamash rewarded their courage by sending mighty winds from heaven against Humbaba. The blasts beat upon him from all directions and hurled him backwards, until he was held trapped against the wall of his own house.

The huge giant thrashed and struggled, but remained pinned to the wall by the force of the wind. Quivering and quaking with fear, he cried, "Have mercy, great Gilgamesh. I swear that if you let me live, I shall become your faithful servant."

But Enkidu shook his head sternly. "Do not listen to the cunning creature," he advised. "If you set him free, you will surely never see Uruk again."

Gilgamesh listened to his friend's wise words. Raising his axe high above his head, he struck Humbaba with all his might. The giant's body hit the ground with an almighty thud, which echoed throughout the great forest for many miles.

Gilgamesh, Enkidu and the warriors returned triumphant to Uruk – not only with the head of Humbaba, but with many felled cedars to make the mighty city of Uruk even stronger.

Gilgamesh's faith in himself paid off. He got his wish and tales are still told of his courageous deed to this very day.

33

The Brave Tin Soldier

Retold from the original tale
by Hans Christian Andersen

ALITTLE BOY WAS once given a box of twenty-five tin soldiers as a gift. They wore smart uniforms and proudly shouldered their guns, and the little boy was very pleased with them. Only one of the tin soldiers wasn't quite perfect, for he had just one leg. He and his brothers had all been made from the same tin spoon, and there hadn't been quite enough metal to finish him off. Still, it was because he stood out as being special that the little boy put him to stand guard at the gates of the toy castle, instead of keeping him in the box with the others.

The tin soldier was very honoured to have been given an important duty, and he stood to attention,

staring straight ahead. His gaze landed on a beautiful tiny doll whom the boy had placed in the open castle doorway. She was made of the very best plastic and wore a ballet dress of thin muslin, tied at the waist with a shiny blue ribbon. She held both her arms gracefully over her head and she balanced beautifully on one leg, for just like the tin soldier, she had one leg missing. (Well, in actual fact that wasn't the truth. The girl's other leg was extended out behind her because she was a dancer. But the tin soldier wasn't in a position to see it.) That would be just the wife for me, the tin soldier thought at least ten times every day. But the tin soldier dared not go and tell the girl of his love for her, for he was on duty.

One morning, the tin soldier was unexpectedly relieved of his post. A sudden breeze blew through the open window causing the curtains to flutter and knocking the soldier right off his feet and over the windowsill. Down he tumbled through the air, until he landed headfirst on the pavement.

The tin soldier didn't cry out for he was brave-

hearted in the face of danger – not even when big drops of rain began to bombard him from above. So this is what it feels like to be out on the battlefield, the brave tin soldier thought.

Eventually the rain stopped falling and two keen-eyed boys came along and spotted the tin soldier among the puddles. The boys quickly folded some newspaper into a boat, popped the tin soldier in the middle, and set him afloat in the rainwater that rushed down the gutter at the side of the street. They ran alongside the boat as it swirled along, cheering it on its way delightedly. The tin soldier was shaking with fear inside, but he didn't flinch or move a muscle – even when the rushing water carried his newspaper boat down a drain and into the darkness under the pavement.

Suddenly a huge water-rat appeared. "Who goes there?" it demanded, twitching its whiskers and baring its long teeth.

'At last, I face the enemy!' thought the brave tin soldier. But before he could lower his gun and aim it, his newspaper boat was carried past the rat on the tide.

A glimmer of light appeared in the distance and the rushing of the water grew louder and louder. The tin

soldier realised with horror that he was being swept towards a sudden drop where the drain water cascaded in a waterfall into a canal below. Even worse, the churning waters were splashing over the sides of the newspaper boat and the bottom was growing soggy beneath the tin soldier's feet. "Steady! Steady! Hold the line!" the brave tin soldier told himself. Suddenly the bottom of the boat ripped and gave way. The tin soldier plunged into the deeps and the icy waters closed over his head.

'Surely now I am done for!' thought the tin soldier, as he sank downwards through the murky wetness. Then all at once, everything went black as a fish swallowed him. The tin soldier choked and spluttered as he was gulped down into the fish's gullet, then the waters drained away and he was left lying on his back, holding tightly onto his gun. Even though the tin soldier couldn't see in the darkness, he could just about breathe in the stinking, rotten air. So this is what it's like to be a prisoner of war in a dungeon, the brave tin soldier thought to himself. To keep up his spirits, he concentrated on the beautiful dancing girl he had left at the castle.

The tin soldier lost track of time inside the fish, but eventually he was flung to and fro as the creature was

caught on a hook
and struggled to
escape. Then everything
went quiet and still for
quite a while, until suddenly
the fish was cut open. "I
don't believe it!" came a voice
"Here's the missing tin soldier," and
a woman with a kind face reached in and pulled him
out. She gave the brave tin soldier a shower under a
running tap, carried him into the drawing room and
set him back in his old position outside his very own
castle.

The tin soldier puffed out his chest with pride. The
war is over. I am back where I belong, he thought to
himself. He stared straight ahead, and there was his
love, his sweetheart, the beautiful little dancing girl.
Tomorrow, as soon as I am off duty, I will definitely ask
her to marry me, the tin soldier decided. But then he
felt an icy wind around his ankles, and a breeze coming
through the window once more swept him off his feet
and into the air. This time he landed in the blazing
flames of the open fire – but the brave tin soldier
didn't mind, for the dancing girl was blown in too and
landed at his side. "Be brave, my love!" cried the tin

soldier, holding his gun on his shoulder, and the dancing girl burst into flames and was gone. Then the tin soldier himself began to melt... and the next day, when the woman with the kind face was raking over the ashes, she found a tiny tin heart that the fire had been unable to burn away.